HATTIE HARMONY

OPENING NIGHT

ELIZABETH OLSEN & ROBBIE ARNETT

ILLUSTRATED BY MARISSA VALDEZ

VIKING

Opening night had arrived . . . and Wildwood Elementary was preparing for the school play. There was still work to be done, and some of the students had a case of the OPENING NIGHT jitters.

Luckily, **HATTIE HARMONY: WORRY DETECTIVE** was ready to help.

BRING BRING

Script for HATTIE

Admit One TICKET

"Hattie, it's Pearl Peppercorn. I have a terrible feeling. I think it's stage fright!"

"Don't you worry, Pearl," Hattie said. "Meet me at the theater. I'll be there just as soon as you can say . . ."

Worry, worry, go away!
There's no time for you today!
It's opening night of
the school
play!

Hattie put on her trusty
Worry Detective Tool Belt.
It was time to get to work.

"Pearl? . . . Pearl? . . . Pearl? . . . Are you here?"
"I'm here, Hattie," Pearl cried. "I think I've forgotten all my lines! What am I going to do?"

Hattie reached in her Tool Belt and grabbed JENNY JOURNAL.

"Sometimes, when we get excited, our brains move super-duper fast and it makes it hard for us to think."

"But, Hattie," said Pearl, "I need to say my lines out loud, not write them down."

"If you give it a try, you might find that journaling can help us understand our feelings and organize our thoughts. I always have my pencil on hand. Why don't you start with 'I feel' and then fill in the blank."

"Hattie, it's working! I can hear myself think!"
"Whenever you're feeling overwhelmed," Hattie
said, "you can always write your feelings down."

"Why don't you keep JENNY JOURNAL," said Hattie.

Then suddenly . . .

BOOM!

A loud noise came from behind the stage curtain.
"OH NO!"

"I ruined my set! I spilled paint everywhere," yelped Seymour Swiggletooth.

"Don't you worry," Hattie said. "We'll make this better just as soon as you can say . . ."

Hattie splashed her tail in the spilled paint
and started to use it as a brush.

"A forest isn't supposed to look like that!" Seymour squealed. "Forests are green!"

"But in the play, the forest can be any color in the whole wide world," Hattie said. "Just use your imagination."

"But what if people don't like it?" asked Seymour. "It needs to be perfect."

"Seymour, there is no such thing as 'perfect.' Every tree is different, just like every one of us is different. That's what makes us special. This set doesn't need to be perfect; it just needs to come from within . . ."

YOU.

"You were right, Hattie. This might be my favorite set EVER!"

"UH-OH!"
"Who turned out all the lights?"
Hattie hollered.

"Whoopsie!" shouted Duncan Delmar.
"And now I can't turn them back on."

Hattie pulled out her trusty FLASHLIGHT and discovered Duncan pressing all the buttons in a panic.

"I'm the director and I can't even turn the lights on. How will anyone be able to see the show?"

"Don't you worry, Duncan," Hattie said. "I'll find the right tool just as soon as you can say . . ."

WORRY, WORRY, GO AWAY! THERE'S NO TIME FOR YOU TODAY!

Hattie pulled out TIMMY TIMER.
"Let me introduce you to my good friend Timmy.
He can remind us to take breaks when things
become too overwhelming," Hattie said. "Come on!"

Hattie and Duncan smelled the tall grass and felt the cool breeze. They used all of their senses to put their minds at ease.

"I feel so much calmer," said Duncan. "A break really *can* help."

Ding!
Ding!

"Why don't you keep TIMMY TIMER. He'll
remind you to take a break when you need it."
"Thank you, Hattie," said Duncan.

"You're welcome. After all, you directors
have a lot on your minds!"

It was almost SHOWTIME!
Everyone lined up onstage in their costumes.

"Um . . . Hattie," squeaked Bonnie Beverley.
"I think I ripped my costume. Can you fix it?"

"Don't you worry. I'll find the right
tool as soon as you can say . . ."

Hattie pulled out SASHA SEWING KIT and got to work.
Suddenly, Hattie's hands started to shake.
"I'm a little nervous about sewing. What if I can't fix it?"
worried Hattie.

"It's okay, just try your best," Bonnie said. "Sometimes
when I get nervous, I take deep, slow breaths, then imagine
I'm in a beautiful, peaceful place. Like the beach!

"Now imagine sand in our hands, the water touching our toes, and the hot, hot sun smiling at us."

"Ah, this is so relaxing! I can hear the waves!

"I didn't know imagining a peaceful place could make you feel peaceful, too. I think I'm ready to stitch your costume now."

Everyone gathered backstage for one last
GOOD-LUCK hug.

"If we feel scared or anxious while we are onstage,"
said Hattie, "just remember, we are all in this together,
and together we can do anything!"

Hattie reached in her Tool Belt and pulled out her
old friend MISS MIRROR so everyone could see their
reflection . . .

WORRY, WORRY, GO AWAY!
THERE'S NO TIME FOR
YOU TODAY!
IT'S OPENING NIGHT
OF THE SCHOOL PLAY!

"Places, everyone," said Duncan.

As the play ended, Hattie and all her friends took a BIG bow.
The audience loved it! But most importantly, everyone had FUN!

Hattie made sure to congratulate all her friends.
Opening night was a success! "Oh, and one more thing,"
Hattie said with a smile. "If you ever need me for anything
at all, you can always call your friend . . ."

AUTHORS' NOTE

Take your places, everyone! Being on "life's stage" can be overwhelming. We are all filled with feelings and emotions—from happy to sad, courageous to fearful, and so many more. Learning how to identify your feelings is the first step to becoming aware of all your emotions, big and small. Everyone needs a little help when it comes to managing emotions like anxiety, so that's why Hattie Harmony uses the tools below and empowering self-talk to soothe many kinds of worries.

As two people who deeply believe in the importance of mindful thinking, we hope the Hattie Harmony series will inspire children to be curious, empathetic, and resilient in an anxious world that has many unknown challenges.

TOOLS USED IN THIS BOOK

JOURNALING: When our worries feel very big, journaling can organize the overwhelming thoughts and make them feel more manageable. It's important to have a safe, private place to express our concerns, to sort through or track them, and ultimately, to better understand them. Hattie encourages Pearl Peppercorn to use Jenny Journal to help her mind slow down when Pearl feels like the world is moving too fast.

CREATIVE SELF-EXPRESSION / CREATIVE THINKING: The creative arts can help us regulate, communicate, and understand our deepest selves better. It's important to remove any judgment so the creative juices can flow! Hattie helps Seymour Swiggletooth see that sometimes what we perceive as a "mistake" can lead to an even more beautiful outcome. The need for something to be perfect adds new layers to an already-stressful situation. By having fun and expressing our individual selves, or reframing our thoughts, we can reduce anxiety.

BRAIN BREAKS: Brain breaks are when people are given a set period of time for a mental time-out. Short, physical bursts (like stretching or exercises like jumping jacks) or a mindful break that uses our senses (touch, hearing, smell, sight, taste) can help kids take a break from their thoughts and reenergize and refocus for more clarity. When Duncan Delmar feels overwhelmed, Hattie sets Timmy Timer so they can move their bodies, use their senses, and feel less stress.

GUIDED IMAGERY: When we use our imaginations to think of positive and happy experiences or beautiful, peaceful places, we bring more awareness to our feelings and our brains can increase levels of endorphins and serotonin—putting us in a more relaxed state. Bonnie Beverley uses breathing with a guided visualization to help Hattie return her mind to a calmer place.

AFFIRMATIONS: Hattie uses affirmations like "Worry, worry, go away!" to replace anxiety-producing thoughts and negative self-talk. These statements can help motivate and inspire us. And the more we repeat them, the more automatic they become.

To Nancy, John, Jarnie, and Dave,
for sitting through many opening nights.
—E. O. and R. A.

For Jessica, Alaine, and Yasmine,
you fill my life with the best kind of drama.
—M. V.

VIKING

An imprint of Penguin Random House LLC, New York

First published in the United States of America by Viking,
an imprint of Penguin Random House LLC, 2023

Text copyright © 2023 by Robert Arnett and Elizabeth Olsen
Illustrations copyright © 2023 by Marissa Valdez

Visit us online at penguinrandomhouse.com.

Library of Congress Cataloging-in-Publication Data is available.

Manufactured in China

ISBN 9780593351468

10   9   8   7   6   5   4   3   2   1

TOPL

Book design by Marissa Valdez and Jim Hoover   Set in Harmonia Sans Pro

The authors wish to thank Dr. Lori Barker, Mrs. Suzie S. Foger, and Dr. Donna DeFazio, LCSW.